For Daisy, Oliver and Piper,
with love – S. M.

To those who encourage
and inspire me – E. J.

FAR
FAR
AWAY
BOOKS

George
and the
Knight

Sue McMillan   Ellie Jenkins

Long ago, when the tallest oaks were nothing more than tiny acorns, brave dragons roamed a distant land.

The dragons were fearsome and mighty,

but George was different.

He did not wish to be fearsome. He was not mighty.

George was kind and gentle.

All the dragons were ashamed of him. They tried and tried to make George brave, but it was no good.

Finally, they decided that George must go.

He was banished from the mountain and told

never to return again.

Alone in the forest, George wandered on and on.

But in time, his hunger drove him to

an orchard overlooking a village.

That is when Alric,

the blacksmith's son, spotted him.

The boy did not run
when he saw the dragon, but gazed in awe
at the beautiful scales and softly whispered,

"Wow!"

George was startled. He let out a puff of grey smoke.
"D-d-d-don't hurt m-m-m-me,"
he stuttered.

"How can you be afraid of me?
I thought dragons were fearless!?"

"I'm afraid of everything."
George blushed.
"And for that reason,
I cannot return home."

"Are you a fire-breathing dragon?" asked Alric.

"Oh yes," replied George. "All dragons are."

"Can you show me?" the boy urged.

George opened his mouth and sent a scorching fire onto a nearby log. It burst into bright, hot flames.

"Amazing!" cried Alric.

"That gives me an idea! Come with me!"

So Alric led George to the village, where his father was hard at work.

The blacksmith was surprised to see a dragon. "Can George stay with us, ple-e-ease?" Alric pleaded. "He can make your fire burn brighter!"

His father laughed.
"A fire-breathing dragon
in the forge?
Well, let's try!"

A plume of fire roared from the dragon's mouth.
It brightened the flames, so the forge burned
more fiercely than ever before.
The blacksmith plunged a piece of metal into the flames.
In seconds, Alric's father held up a magnificent sword.

Alric let out a long whistle.
"It's the best you've ever made!"

The villagers were happy.

They were proud to have a dragon and proud of their blacksmith, who became known far and wide for all the **wonderful** things he made with George's magical fire.

It seemed that life could not be better, until one day the king sent a new knight to the castle. The villagers lined the streets to greet him.

But when he arrived they all gasped!

"Oh no!
It's Lord
Badwick!"

Badwick was known throughout the land as a selfish, cruel knight and a slithering, eye-piercing, bloodthirsty, ruthless, dragon-hunter.

George was in great danger!

And so, before the sun appeared, George, Alric and his father flew to a secret cave where the gentle dragon could hide from the wicked knight.

The cave was cold and dark.

Alric did not want to leave his friend

in such a gloomy place, but he knew

that it was far better than facing Badwick.

Holding back his tears,
Alric hugged George tightly,

not knowing when he would see him again.

They sadly waved goodbye.

Badwick's cruelty made the villagers wretched.

This wicked knight took everything they had.

When winter came, he would not let them
gather wood in the forest.

Without firewood, they shivered in the cold.
But he did not care at all.

All Badwick cared about was eating.
He ate and ate ... all day long.

More than anything else, Badwick craved his favourite meal,
spicy hot dragon wings and toast
with clawberry jam!

"I must go dragon-hunting NOW.

Fetch me my armour,"

he commanded.

But his armour did not fit. He huffed and he puffed, he squeezed and he moaned, but it was no use.

He had grown too fat.

"Bring me the blacksmith!" he shouted.

"I must have new armour!"

The blacksmith was forced to go to the castle.
When he returned he gathered the villagers at the well.
"I must make new armour for Badwick to go dragon-hunting,"
he explained.

"We must save George!" Alric cried.

"How can you think of dragons
when we are starving?" said the baker, angrily.

"Wait," said the blacksmith,
"I have a plan.

This could be our only chance. If George warns the other dragons, we can all fight together. Then we can stop Badwick for good!

George is our only hope."

Alric hurried away to tell George.

When Alric reached the cave, he hardly recognized George.
The sad dragon looked very small and scared.

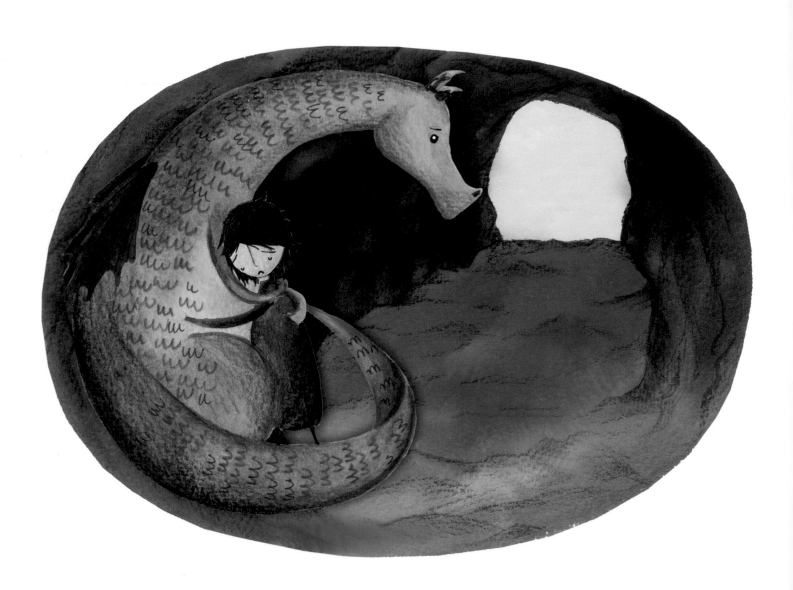

However, the two friends were so happy to meet again
that they held each other tightly without uttering a word.
At last Alric spoke. He told George the news.

GEORGE'S eyes widened.

He was very afraid to go
back to the mountain, but he
knew he must warn the
other dragons and help his friends.
Pushing away his fear, George soared
into the sky with Alric upon his back.

Down in the village,
the blacksmith worked and worked,
day and night, to complete the armour.

When it was ready, Badwick tried to put it on.

"This armour is TOO SMALL!"

he thundered.

"Blacksmith! You will not leave this castle until the armour fits!"

Meanwhile, George and Alric
arrived at the mountain.

An ear-splitting roar
shook the ground and fire melted the
snow-covered peak.

It was Cruncher,
the fierce dragon ruler.

Plumes of fire shot from his mouth.

Smoke curled from his nostrils.

He flashed his gleaming
teeth in anger.

George wrapped a protective tail
around Alric.

"Why are you here? You are banished!"

Cruncher roared, furious that George had dared to return.

George tried to explain.

"You are all in grave d-d-d-danger!" he stuttered.

"Danger?" roared Cruncher with a huge, booming laugh. "Leave, before I turn you into toast! NOW!"

George looked the old dragon straight in the eye.

"No," he said, "I won't leave. Lord Badwick plans to kill us all. We must go to the village at once."

"So, George, there is fire in your belly," chuckled Cruncher.

"I am proud of you.

It took courage to come here.

Gather the dragons. Badwick

must be defeated."

The sky filled with dragons.

They followed George and Alric to the village, where everyone was waiting. The baker ran towards Alric. "Lord Badwick has your father," he said breathlessly. "He won't let him go until he finishes the armour."

"We must hurry," Alric replied urgently.
The villagers climbed on the dragons' backs
and flew straight to the castle.

The battle had begun!

Lord Badwick's army was fierce

and confident. But it was no match for

the angry villagers and fiery dragons.

Soon, the cruel knight's men were clutching their

burning bottoms and running away!

George and Alric searched for the blacksmith. Finally, they spotted him.

Alric ran to greet his father.

Just then, a wicked laugh boomed from the shadows. Badwick!

"You ruined my plans, blacksmith!"

As Lord Badwick drew his sword, Alric picked up
the blacksmith's hammer and swung it at him.
"You are a brave but foolish boy!" sneered Badwick.

"And your dragon is a coward!"

With a belly full of fire
and a will **to save Alric** and his father,

George rose into the sky.

"I am not a coward!"

The mighty dragon swooped upon them with a blast of fire,
melting Badwick's sword into nothing. Then he roared again
and swept Alric up onto his back.

"Help!" squealed the terrified knight
as George grabbed him by his fat little toes
and flew up into the sky.

When George reached the royal palace he went straight to the King.

There, he dropped the plump, whining, whimpering, wicked Badwick.

The King listened to Alric's story with a grave face.

Lord Badwick had been sent to care for his village and its people.

Now they were **cold** and **hungry**

because of his greedy selfishness.

Badwick snivelled quietly as
the King spoke.
"Take him
away!"

The villagers rejoiced!

Badwick was gone for good!

Dragons and villagers feasted
and celebrated for many weeks.

Forever after, that day was called
Dragon Day.

Somewhere in the mountains of

a faraway kingdom,

high above the tallest oaks,

mighty dragons live happily
thanks to George,

the bravest dragon

of all.

The End

... and George?

Cruncher asked him to return to the mountain.

But the gentle dragon wanted nothing more than to live peacefully in the village with his friends.

And there he stayed.

Many thanks to Moira Butterfield,

Vicki Talbot and Richard Trenchard.

for working their

editing magic.

First published in Great Britain in 2012
by Far Far Away Books and Media Ltd.
20-22 Bedford Row, London WC1R 4JS

ISBN: 978-1-908786-04-3 (hardback)
ISBN: 978-1-908786-62-3 (paperback)

A CIP catalogue record for this book is
available from the British Library.

Designed at www.aitchcreative.co.uk

Printed and bound in Portugal
by Printer Portuguesa

FSC
www.fsc.org

MIX
Paper from
responsible sources
FSC® C006423

www.farfarawaybooks.com